D0229719

BRENT LIBRARIES

Please return/renew this item
by the last date shown.
Books may also be renewed by
phone or online.
Tel: 0333 370 4700
On-line www.brent.gov.uk/libraryservice

LAURA OWEN & KORKY PAUL

OXFORD

Helping your child to read

Before they start

* Talk about the back cover blurb. What kind of problems do you think Winnie might have with her new 'kitten'?
* Look at the picture on the cover. Does it give any clues about what might happen in the stories?

During reading

* Let your child read at their own pace, either silently or out loud.
* If necessary, help them to work out words they don't know by saying each sound out loud and then blending them to say the word, e.g. *p-o-ng-b-e-rr-y, pongberry*.

* Encourage your child to keep checking that the text makes sense and they understand what they are reading. Remind them to reread to check the meaning if they're not sure.
* Give them lots of praise for good reading!

After reading

* Look at page 48 for some fun activities.

Contents

Winnie's New Kitten ... 5

Winnie's Lost Teddy ... 25

OXFORD
UNIVERSITY PRESS

Great Clarendon Street, Oxford OX2 6DP

Oxford University Press is a department of the University of Oxford.
It furthers the University's objective of excellence in research, scholarship,
and education by publishing worldwide. Oxford is a registered trade mark
of Oxford University Press in the UK and in certain other countries

"Winnie's New Kitten" was first published in *Winnie the Bold* 2015
"Winnie's Lost Teddy" was first published in *Winnie's Alien Sleepover* 2015
This edition published 2019

British Library Cataloguing in Publication Data

Data available

ISBN: 978-0-19-276920-6

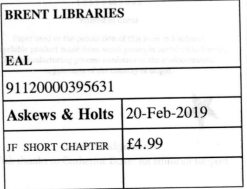

Winnie's
New Kitten

✦ Chapter ✦ One

Winnie wanted to play a game. "Hey, Wilbur, catch this!" she said, throwing a pongberry towards him. But Wilbur didn't leap up and catch the berry. In fact, he didn't even open his eyes or twitch his whiskers. The pongberry bounced off his head. **Ping! Snore**, he went. **SNORE!**

"You're no fun any more!" said Winnie.

Winnie tickled Wilbur behind his ear.
"Play with me, Wilbur," she said. "Pleeease?
If you play with me, I'll cook you fish
fingers. I'll even cook you fish toes!" But
Wilbur just carried on snoring.

Winnie sighed. "When you were a kitten,
you played all the time. You were as fun as
a bun on the run! But now you're old and
grumpy and boring."

SNORE!

"I know!" said Winnie. "I think I'll get myself a new kitten!"

Suddenly, Wilbur woke up.

"Meeow!" he said. He meant, "I thought you loved me."

But Winnie had made up her mind.

"The new kitten won't be *instead of* you," Winnie told him. "It will be *as well as* you. After all, we've got lots of room."

"Meeow!" said Wilbur, crossly this time.

But Winnie took her wand from her pocket,

and was just about to say a spell, when . . .

Brriiiinnnnggg! Wiiiinnnniiiieeee!

went the doorbell.

"Who can that be?" said Winnie, opening

the door.

A man in a cap was standing on the
doorstep. There was a big box beside him.

"Err, I think I might be in the wrong
place," said the man, scratching his head.
"You don't look like a zookeeper. Are you
expecting a parcel of a feline kind?"

"I don't know," said Winnie. "What is a
'feline kind'?"

"'Feline' means 'cat'," said the delivery man. "I have a young feline in this box here."

"Oh, that's perfect!" said Winnie, clapping her hands together. "Purr-fect, in fact! And you were so quick, too!"

"Just sign here," said the man, tapping his foot and looking at his watch.

So Winnie quickly signed her name.

⭐ Chapter Two

Winnie pulled the box inside, and shut the door. "Do you want to open it, Wilbur, or shall I?" she asked.

Wilbur just scowled.

So Winnie opened the box – and out leaped a big, beautiful, stripy young cat!

"Oooh, look, Wilbur!" said Winnie. "Isn't he handsome?"

Hisss! went Wilbur.

"Oh, don't be as mean as a cross baked bean, Wilbur. He's only a baby!"

Winnie stroked her new kitten, tickling gently behind his ear.

PURRRR! went the kitten loudly.

"You're the same pattern as my tights," said Winnie. "So that's what I'll call you."

Then Tights jumped down and opened the cupboard door, and then the fridge door . . .

He ate *everything*!

After that, Tights jumped up onto the worktop, turned on the tap with his paw, and drank *all* the water in the sink. Then he looked at Winnie hungrily.

"Oh dear!" said Winnie. "I'd better find you something else to eat." Winnie took out her wand. But before she could wave it, Tights pounced on the wand. **CRASH!**

"That's nice!" said Winnie rather nervously. "He wants to play!" She found a fluffy slipper with long ribbons, and tied it to the end of her wand. Then she dangled the slipper in front of Tights.

Tights was growling. He was prowling. He was about to pounce . . .

Suddenly, Winnie started to feel a little bit frightened. "Wilbur!" she shouted.

Wilbur didn't answer straight away. He was busy. He'd gone to the bookshelf and picked out a book called *The Big Book of Animals*. When he got to the 'T' page he held it up to show Winnie . . .

"A *tiger?*" said Winnie. "You mean, Tights is a t-t-t-t-tiger?"

Pounce! Chomp!

⭐ Chapter ⭐ Three

Tights chomped the slipper and the ribbon —
and half of Winnie's wand. Luckily, Wilbur
had a plan. He pointed to the empty
food cupboard.

"Meeow!" he said, meaning, "Hurry!"

Winnie ran inside, and Wilbur slammed
the door to keep her safe. **Pounce!** Tights
went to try to catch Wilbur.

Wilbur was too fast for Tights the tiger. He zipped out of the kitchen, through the cat flap. Tights was too big to follow him.

Winnie was trapped in the food cupboard, but at least she was safe from Tights!

"Oooh," said Winnie nervously. All she could do was wait inside the cupboard, sitting on a shelf like a tin of baked beans.

"Meeow!" Wilbur was on his way to get help. He used a vine to swing over the garden wall to visit Jerry, the giant who lived next door.

"Meeow!" said Wilbur to Jerry and his dog Scruff. He acted out what had happened to poor Winnie.

"What? Winnie needs me?" said Jerry, and he, Wilbur and Scruff ran over to Winnie's house.

With one giant kick, Jerry bashed down
Winnie's door. **CRASH!** He picked up Tights
the tiger . . . who suddenly looked as little
as a kitten in Jerry's great big hands. Tights
looked a little bit scared now, too.

Wilbur opened the cupboard door, and
Winnie wobbled out.

"Oooh, thank you, Wilbur and Jerry and
Scruff!" she said in a wobbly voice. "Er, I
think we should take Tights to the zoo."

So they all went along the road to the zoo. The zookeeper was so happy to see Tights that he gave them a reward.

"You can all have free rides," he said. "I'll just pop our little baby tiger in with the big tigers."

Then Jerry rode an elephant, Wilbur and Scruff rode in baskets on either side of a zebra and Winnie rode a camel.

"Just one more thing!" said Winnie,
and she waved her wand. "**Abracadabra!**"
Instantly, they all had enormous ice creams.

"This treat is because of you, Wilbur,"
said Winnie. "So you *do* make things fun
after all!"

Winnie and Wilbur were tired and full of ice cream when they got home, so they went straight to bed.

Just as Winnie's eyes closed she said, "When you were a kitten, Wilbur, you always wanted to play . . . even at bedtime." **Yawn!** "I'm glad that you're a grown-up cat now, not a kitten."

Purrr! went Wilbur.

Winnie's Lost Teddy

✦ Chapter ✦
One

Snip-snap! Snip-snap!

Winnie's croc alarm clock was trying to wake her up.

"Wh-what's up?" said Winnie, sitting up in bed.

"Meeow," muttered Wilbur. He was holding on to the very edge of the bed. He hadn't slept at all well. Winnie and her teddy bear took up all the space in bed.

Yawn! Winnie flung her arms out wide
and stretched. But she ended up punching
Wilbur right out of bed. **Bump!** Winnie
didn't even notice. She was too busy hugging
her teddy bear, and talking to him. "What
a cuddly friend you are, old Beddy-Teddy!"
she said.

Wilbur scowled.

Brriiiinnnnggg! Wiiiinnnniiiieeee!
yelled the doorbell.

"Who's that at the door?" said Winnie,
pulling on her dressing gown.

Wilbur stamped down the stairs.

29

Creak! He opened the door.

"Good morning!" said Mrs Parmar. She was standing on the doorstep with two of the children from school. "We are collecting jumble for the sale at school tomorrow. Do you have any nice jumble for us, Winnie?"

"Oooh, I'm sure I can find you some bits and bobs," said Winnie.

30

"Now, where did I put that make-your-wellies-smell-nice machine that Auntie Aggie gave me for my birthday?" she said. "I've never used it, and I never will."

"That sounds lovely!" said Mrs Parmar, sounding surprised. "Perhaps you've also got some old toys?"

Winnie wasn't listening. She had her head in a cupboard, looking for the make-your-wellies-smell-nice machine. But Wilbur had heard what Mrs Parmar said, and it gave him a very, very, very wicked idea.

Quickly, sneakily, Wilbur ran up the stairs and into the bedroom. He snatched Beddy-Teddy, and then slid silently down the bannisters.

⭐ Chapter ⭐
Two

Before Winnie could see, Wilbur popped Beddy-Teddy into the jumble box. He stood in front of it to hide what he had done.

"Here it is!" said Winnie, pulling out a huge box. "Urgh! It smells of rosy-posies even when it's not switched on. I'll be glad to be rid of it."

Wilbur stepped forward. He lifted the
box into the crate of jumble, on top of
Beddy-Teddy.

"Oooh, thank you, Wilbur, you're such a
gentleman!" said Winnie. Wilbur looked
at the floor. "And you're modest, too!"
she added.

Mrs Parmar and the children went off
with their box.

Winnie and Wilbur had a normal sort
of day after that, except that Wilbur kept
helping Winnie with everything.

"You're being very good today," said
Winnie. She didn't realise he was feeling
very guilty about something.

After supper Winnie had a bath (and Wilbur scrubbed her back). Then she put on her nightie, cleaned her teeth (Wilbur had squeezed the toothpaste for her) and jumped into bed (Wilbur had already plumped up all her pillows).

"Come on, Wilbur, it's beddy-byes time," said Winnie.

So Wilbur jumped on to the bed, too. He
lay there with his eyes wide open. There
was lots of lovely room, but Wilbur wasn't
happy . . . and, soon, neither was Winnie.

"Where's my cuddly-as-a-puddly old
Beddy-Teddy gone?" she said.

"Meeow?" Wilbur tried to look innocent.

Winnie looked under the bed. She looked in the bed. She looked around the room. She looked around the house. She looked around the garden.

"I can't sleep without my Beddy-Teddy," said Winnie. "Oh, I'll just have to make myself a new teddy bear."

So Winnie made a bear out of some old tights, stuffed with the insides of a cushion.

"Oh, no! It looks more like a snake, and it's not going to give me sweet dreams!" she sobbed.

"Meeow?" sighed Wilbur. He handed Winnie her wand.

"Of course!" said Winnie. "Wilbur, you are not just a gentleman cat, you are also a genius cat! I'll magic my dear old Beddy-Teddy back." Winnie waved her wand. "Abracadabra!"

⭐ Chapter ⭐
Three

Growl, growl!

There *was* a bear, but it was hairier and scarier than Beddy-Teddy used to be!

"Er, oh my. How you've grown, Beddy-Teddy!" said Winnie. The great big bear picked Winnie up as if she was *its* toy, and then snuggled into bed – **creak!** – then went to sleep. Winnie was still wide awake!

"Meeow!" said Wilbur. It was all his
fault! Wilbur knew that he must get the *real*
Beddy-Teddy back. Quickly!

Wilbur put on a cat-burglar mask, rushed
out of the house, and hurried down the dark
streets to the school.

Everything was dark, dark . . . except for a spark of light that came from inside the school. Wilbur peered in through the window. "Meeow?" he said in surprise.

A burglar was running away with the head teacher's laptop and Mrs Parmar's tin of toffees! The burglar looked just like the snake Winnie had made — her magic had brought it to life! Wilbur opened the window and pounced on the burglar. **Leap! Hiss!**

"Meeow!" Wilbur told him sternly, sitting on his tummy and holding him down. Then he used the burglar's mobile phone to text the police. **Bleep! Bleep! Bloop!**

Wilbur saw Beddy-Teddy on a table with some other toys for sale. So, quick as a flick of his tail, Wilbur grabbed Beddy-Teddy. He escaped out of the window, just as the police arrived to put on some handcuffs.

Wilbur held Beddy-Teddy tight in his teeth, and hurried all the way home. He had to rescue Winnie from the big hairy scary bear! Was Winnie still all right?

She was! The spell didn't last long. The big hairy scary bear had disappeared. And Winnie was fast asleep, clutching her wand.

"Meeow!" sighed Wilbur happily. He took off his mask and tucked Beddy-Teddy in next to Winnie. Then he snuggled in beside them. **Wallop!** Winnie moved her arm in her sleep, pushing Wilbur to the very edge of the bed. But he didn't mind.

Zzzz!

In the morning, Winnie said, "I had a strange dream last night, Wilbur. I dreamed that there was a real bear in my bedroom. Can you imagine? And then . . . oh, my giddy goodness me, look, Wilbur! I've just found my old Beddy-Teddy!" And she hugged Beddy-Teddy. "Silly me," she said. "He wasn't lost at all!"

Wilbur didn't say anything.

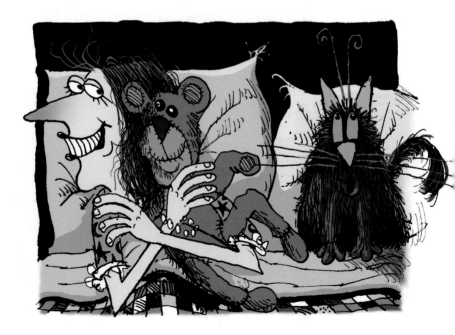

At the jumble sale, everyone was talking about the burglar who had been caught in the school the night before.

"Fancy stealing other people's things! That's as nasty as filling somebody's bed full of slugs!" said Winnie.

"Meeow," said Wilbur, nodding his head.

Guess what Winnie bought at the jumble sale? A funny old teddy bear for Wilbur. So now there's even less room in their bed than before!

After reading activities

Quick quiz

See how fast you can answer these
questions! Look back at the stories if
you can't remember.

1) In "Winnie's New Kitten", why does
   Winnie decide to call the tiger Tights?
2) In "Winnie's Lost Teddy", what does
   Winnie give to the jumble sale (besides
   Beddy-Teddy)?
3) In "Winnie's Lost Teddy", what
   happens when Winnie tries to magic
   Beddy-Teddy back?

1) because it's stripy like her tights; 2) a make-your-wellies-smell-
nice machine; 3) she gets a giant hairy scary bear instead

Try this!

 ⋆ Winnie and Wilbur's bed is a bit
   crowded and there's not much room for
   them or their teddies. Design and draw
   a beautiful new witchy bed for Winnie
   and Wilbur. What cool witchy features
   can you give it?